WHY CAN'T YOU UNSCRAMBLE AN EGG?

BY VICKI COBB, WITH ILLUSTRATIONS BY TED ENIK

Why Doesn't the Earth Fall Up?
and other not such dumb questions about motion

ALSO BY VICKI COBB

Fuzz Does It!
Gobs of Goo
Lots of Rot
The Monsters Who Died
More Power to You!
The Scoop on Ice Cream
Skyscraper Going Up!
Sneakers Meet Your Feet
The Trip of a Drip

WHY CAN'T YOU UNSCRAMBLE AN EGG?

and other not such dumb questions about matter

BY VICKI COBB

with illustrations by Ted Enik

LODESTAR BOOKS   DUTTON   NEW YORK

for Ursula Higgins

Text copyright © 1990 by Vicki Cobb
Illustrations copyright © 1990 by Ted Enik

Library of Congress Cataloging-in-Publication Data

Cobb, Vicki.
   Why can't you unscramble an egg?: and other not such dumb
questions about matter / by Vicki Cobb; illustrated by Ted Enik.
      p.   cm.
   Summary: Answers nine questions about matter, such as why does an
ice cube float?, how much does air weigh?, how does wood burn? and
other concepts about the nature of matter.
    ISBN 0-525-67293-1
   1. Matter—Composition—Juvenile literature. [1. Matter.
2. Questions and answers.] I. Enik, Ted, ill. II. Title.
QC173.36.C63 1990   89-33465
530—dc20   CIP
                                            AC

Published in the United States by Lodestar Books,
an affiliate of Dutton Children's Books,
a division of Penguin Books USA Inc.

Published simultaneously in Canada by
Fitzhenry & Whiteside Limited, Toronto

Editor: Virginia Buckley
Printed in the U.S.A.   First Edition
10 9 8 7 6 5 4 3 2 1

Contents

Which Weighs More, a Pound of Feathers or a Pound of Gold?

Of course a pound of feathers and a pound of gold weigh exactly the same! But if you held a pound of gold in one hand and a pound of feathers in the other, the gold would feel heavier. Your sense of touch can fool you. The feathers take up a lot more space than the gold. You expect something that is larger to weigh more than something that is smaller, so when it doesn't, the smaller object feels heavier.

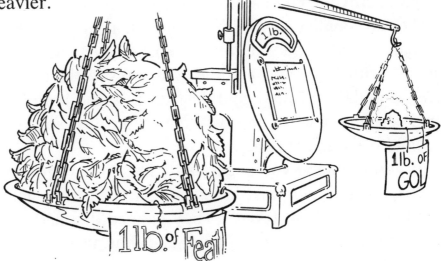

Gold is much denser than feathers. Density is the amount of material, or matter, that is packed into a certain space or volume. If you could pack the feathers into the same volume as the gold, they would have exactly the same density. The feathers would feel as heavy as the gold.

Gold is a very dense metal. A gold chain will feel a lot heavier than one that is not made of gold. See for yourself. Lift gold jewelry. Then lift jewelry that seems to take up the same amount of space but is made of different materials.

Gold is one of the densest kinds of matter on earth. Its density makes it easy to collect from dirt or sand by panning. Anyone can pan for gold. All you do is mix the sand or dirt containing gold with water in a pan. You swish the pan around. The sand or dirt washes over the side of the pan with the water, and the gold sinks to the bottom. Even tiny flakes, called gold dust, sink to the bottom. If you keep adding water and swishing off the dirt, soon only the gold is left in the pan.

If you're lucky, you might find a flake or two in a pan of dirt. When gold was discovered in California, many people caught "gold fever." They panned day and night to collect gold dust. They found gold, but many of them did not get rich.

The densest material in the universe is a black hole. A black hole is not really a hole. It is the densest kind of matter. A piece of black hole the size of a pea would weigh more than the entire earth!

How Can You Make Gold?

You can't make gold. Plain and simple. But hundreds of years ago, some people believed that you could make gold out of other metals, like iron or copper. So they mixed and stirred and heated all kinds of things. They discovered that the only way to end up with gold was to start with gold. They couldn't make gold from anything else because gold is one of the simplest materials on earth. It is an *element*.

There are ninety-two elements in nature. Maybe you already know some of them. Here are a few examples: silver, oxygen, nitrogen, hydrogen, carbon, iron, and neon. Imagine chopping up an element into smaller and smaller pieces. The smallest piece you can get of an element is an *atom*. Atoms are so incredibly tiny that it's hard to imagine how small they are. If you can imagine how many grains of sand there are on a beach, then that's how many atoms there are in a single grain of sand! Gold is a very dense element because its atoms are packed close together.

The people who tried to make gold discovered many other elements besides gold. They also learned that elements can come together and form completely new materials. Elements are like the letters of the alphabet, which combine to make words. For example, iron can combine with oxygen in the air to form a red powder. You know this red powder as *rust*. The smallest part of rust is made up of iron and oxygen atoms. Whenever two or more atoms are combined, a *molecule* is formed. Molecules are bigger than atoms, but they are still incredibly small. Rust is made of molecules, and it is not an element. It is called a *compound*.

Elements combine to form compounds in a ch[e]
reaction. For example, hydrogen reacts with oxygen[?]
form water. This reaction is so strong that there is a[n]
explosion. Compounds can also react with one another to
make different compounds. The science that discovered
elements, compounds, and chemical reactions is called
chemistry.

Water gets larger when it freezes. See for yourself. Fill a paper or Styrofoam cup so that it is half full of water. Hold the cup up to the light so that you can see the water level. Mark the water level on the outside of the cup with a pen. Put the cup in the freezer. Check the level of the water after it has frozen. It is slightly higher than your mark. The ice is larger than the water; therefore ice is less dense than water. The same amount of matter in a larger volume is less dense than in a smaller volume. And anything that is less dense than water will float in it.

It's a good thing for us that ice floats. If all the floating ice at the North and South poles sank into the sea, the oceans would rise and cover all of the land on earth. There would be no place for us to live.

Freezing water can do damage. A closed glass jar full of water can crack when the water freezes and expands. Freezing water in the cracks of a stone makes the cracks larger. This is one way stone is slowly turned into sand. Ice can cause concrete to develop cracks. Cracks are put into sidewalks so they won't form cracks where we don't want them. Ice can also make a road buckle into bumps called frost heaves.

Liquid water can flow from one place to another. It has no special shape. It takes the shape of its container. When water becomes ice, it changes from a liquid to a solid. Ice, like all solids, has its own shape. Water changes to ice when the temperature drops to thirty-two degrees Fahrenheit or zero degrees Celsius. When the temperature is around the freezing point you need to bundle up before going outside.

Other compounds and elements can change from liquids to solids, and then melt and change back from solids to liquids. Gold melts at the very hot temperature of almost 2,000 degrees Fahrenheit or 1,093 degrees Celsius. Candle wax melts at about 125 degrees F or 51 degrees C. That's a little too hot to touch.

The solids of most materials are denser and take up less space than their liquids. Solid gold would sink in melted gold. Water is special. It is one of the few kinds of matter on earth that takes up more space when it is a solid than when it is a liquid.

How Much Does Air Weigh?

Because you can't see or smell or taste it, air seems to be nothing. But it is a kind of matter. It is just not a very dense kind of matter. And like all matter, air does have weight. How can you tell? When it moves as wind, air can destroy houses and uproot trees. If air weighed nothing, it could not move with a force that can do damage.

It's easy to see that air has weight. Get two balloons that are the same size. Blow them up to equal size and hang one at each end of a yardstick. Balance the yardstick in the middle on your fingers. Have a friend stick a pin in one balloon. Can you explain why the yardstick suddenly tilts?

Air is a kind of matter called a *gas*. Actually, air is a mixture of several gases, including nitrogen and oxygen. Gases are like liquids because they can flow from one place to another. They also take the shape of their container. But gases fill a container completely no matter how big or small it is. Liquids don't always do this.

Air completely covers the earth the way egg white surrounds a yolk. The weight of this air pushes on everything and is called *air pressure*. You can use air pressure to do a trick. Air pressure will hold down a wooden yardstick so that you can break it with a karate chop.

Here's how to do it. Place a wooden yardstick on a smooth table so that the end is sticking out about four inches past the edge. Spread two open sheets of newspaper over the yardstick on the table. Smooth down the newspaper so that it hugs the yardstick and tabletop.

Quickly bring your fist down on the part of the stick that is sticking out. You can break it with a single blow. When you move quickly, no air gets under the paper fast enough to make the air pressure underneath equal to the pressure on the surface. Air pressure holds down the paper on the yardstick long enough for you to crack it with your bare hand.

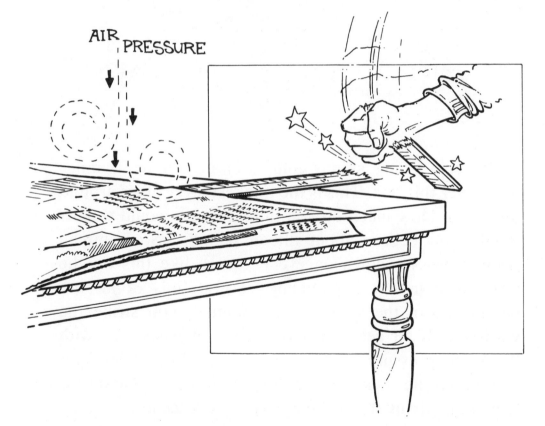

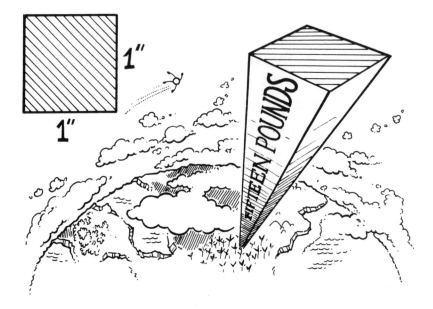

Imagine a long, skinny column of air, five or six miles high, over this box. This is the thickest layer of air around the earth. How much do you think that air would weigh? Would you believe about fifteen pounds? So if fifteen pounds presses down on every square like this on the newspaper in our experiment, several tons of air are holding down the paper at the moment you strike the yardstick. If air gets under the paper, it pushes up with the same pressure as it pushes down. Then the paper won't hold the stick in place. So you have to strike quickly without giving the air time to rush underneath.

Why Don't You Feel Air Pressure?

You can't feel air pressure because the pressure inside your body pushing out is exactly the same as the air from the outside pressing in. So the pressure inside your body cancels out the pressure outside your body. But there are times when you *can* feel a change in air pressure. Here's why.

Air is thickest at sea level. It gets thinner as you go up. As air gets less dense, air pressure drops. So air pressure goes down as you go up. When this happens, your body pressure pushes out and your ears feel clogged. You can feel the change in air pressure when you go up or down in an airplane or elevator. By swallowing, you change the pressure in your ears to make it the same as the outside air pressure.

What would happen if there were suddenly no air pressure? There is no air pressure where there is no air. There is no air on the moon or in space. On earth, air can be pumped out of a space to make a vacuum. If you were suddenly put in a vacuum, your inside pressure would make you swell up until you burst like a balloon.

25

How Is Warm Air Different from Cold Air?

When you heat air, it expands and takes up more space. So warm air is less dense than colder air and rises above it. Unequal heating makes air move.

You can see warm air rising over a stove. Air rising up a chimney draws the flames upward. Hot air balloons trap heated air and carry passengers up into the sky.

If air expands when it is heated, will it shrink when it is cooled? Experiment and find out. Blow up three identical balloons so they are all the same size. Put one in the freezer, one in the refrigerator, and leave one in the kitchen. After two hours, put all three balloons side by side. Which one is the biggest and which one is the smallest?

What happens when air is heated in a closed container? If the heated air can't expand, it pushes harder and harder on the walls of the container. In other words, as the temperature goes up, so does the pressure. If the pressure becomes too strong for the container, there will be an explosion.

TO AVOID EXPLOSIONS, ALWAYS PUT A HOLE IN A CAN BEFORE YOU HEAT IT OVER A CAMPFIRE.

NOW I KNOW WHY THE ATTIC IS SO HOT IN SUMMER.

IF YOU ARE STUCK IN A HOT ATTIC, THE AIR IS COOLER NEAR THE FLOOR.

Why Isn't the Earth Egg-Shaped or a Cube?

The shape of the earth, sun, moon, and stars tells us a lot about matter. These bodies are all shaped like balls. They are called *spheres*. The first thing to remember about each of these bodies is that they contain atoms and molecules that attracted each other. If they hadn't attracted each other, these tiny particles could not have amassed the large collection of matter needed to become what they are now—an earth or moon.

The second thing to remember about a sphere is that at one time its matter was a fluid, which could flow and become the shape it now has. A fluid takes the shape of a sphere. See for yourself. Put some salad oil in an empty olive or mayonnaise jar. Fill the jar up to an inch below the top. Put drops of food coloring into the oil. Put in big drops and little drops. Watch as they all form spheres and sink slowly to the bottom. Beautiful! At the bottom, the drops flatten out because of gravity. But as long as there are no other forces acting on the drops, they will always be spheres.

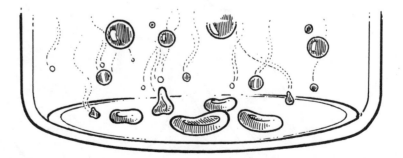

Screw on the top of the jar. Give one hard shake. Now you have broken up the water into hundreds of drops. Can you find one hanging in the oil that is not a sphere?

The sphere is nature's most perfect shape. It contains the most volume in the smallest surface. But the earth is not a perfect sphere. The earth spins like a top, and this makes the earth flatter at the poles and wider at the middle.

Oil and water are two kinds of liquids that don't mix. Shake and shake and all you will make are *millions* of tiny drops.

How Does Wood Burn?

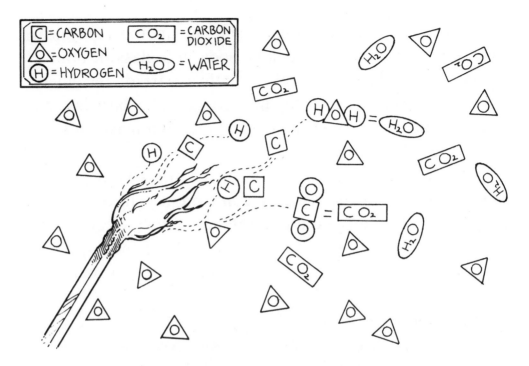

When wood burns, it seems to disappear. But it really doesn't. It changes into other forms of matter. Burning is a chemical reaction. Wood is made up mostly of very large molecules of carbon and hydrogen. When wood burns, the molecules break up. Then the carbon and hydrogen atoms react with oxygen in the air to make carbon dioxide and water. During this reaction, lots of energy is given off as heat and light. The carbon dioxide and water disappear into the air. And the part of the wood that doesn't burn is left behind as ashes.

You can make carbon dioxide in another chemical reaction. Put a pinch of baking soda in a glass of orange juice. The baking soda reacts with a part of the juice. Bubbles form and rise to the surface. The bubbles are carbon dioxide gas. This chemical reaction makes a kind of orange soda.

There are zillions of chemical reactions taking place everywhere. Lots of them are going on in your own body right now. In fact, you are a walking factory of chemical reactions. The oxygen you breathe and the food you eat go through chemical reactions to give you energy and help

you grow. Whenever there is a chemical reaction, the matter you end up with is very different from the matter you started with. Can you name some chemical reactions?

Why Can't You Unscramble an Egg?

Eggs are made up of very large, delicate molecules called *proteins*. Egg protein molecules are like tiny balls of yarn. Beating eggs to scramble them unravels the molecules. It would be impossible to wind them back up. When you heat the egg, there is a chemical reaction. The egg white changes from a clear goo into a white solid. This change is permanent. It happens when the egg is boiled or poached or fried as well as scrambled.

All living things are made of proteins, including you. Proteins are the most important kinds of molecules for life. Proteins help you move and grow and use energy to do all the things you do. When proteins get cooked, they can't do their jobs. That's what happens if you are burned, even sunburned. Proteins are made in your body by chemical reactions. Your body must keep up its supply of proteins and make new ones as you grow.

The challenge of the mystery of life is to try to understand how chemical reactions in living things work. Scientists understand some of them. Here's one for you. Your saliva changes a cracker into sugar. The part of the cracker the saliva works on is not sweet. It is called a starch. Chew a saltine. Hold the chewed cracker in your mouth. Stir it with your tongue. After a while it will start tasting sweet. The saliva has changed the starch into sugar. Saliva contains a special protein, called an *enzyme*, that changes starch to sugar. If you couldn't change starch to sugar, you couldn't get energy from carbohydrates.

If there were no chemical reactions, there would be no life on earth.

Index